Pretty Pebble
NECKLACES

For Bunny, Chicken, and Mouse

Visit us on the Web!
randomhouse.com/kids

Educators and librarians, for a variety of teaching tools,
visit us at RHTeachersLibrarians.com

Visit Penny at myprettypenny.com

Library of Congress Cataloging-in-Publication Data
Kinch, Devon.
Pretty Penny makes ends meet / Devon Kinch. — 1st ed.
p. cm.
Summary: Penny and her pet pig, Iggy, make and sell jewelry in hopes of giving
money to her grandmother, Bunny, who needs to pay for plumbing repairs.
ISBN 978-0-375-86737-8 (trade) — ISBN 978-0-375-96735-1 (lib. bdg.) —
ISBN 978-0-375-98128-9 (ebook)
[1. Moneymaking projects—Fiction. 2. Jewelry making—Fiction.
3. Handicraft—Fiction. 4. Pigs—Fiction.]
I. Title.
PZ7.K5653Pm 2013
[E]—dc23 2012009179

MANUFACTURED IN CHINA
10 9 8 7 6 5 4 3 2 1
First Edition

Pretty Penny Makes Ends Meet

DEVON KINCH

RANDOM HOUSE NEW YORK

It's bedtime at Bunny's house. Penny tucks in Iggy and Bo for the night.

She opens a book and begins to read to them, but suddenly they hear a loud *BOOM!* followed by an even louder *WHOOSH!*

Penny jumps out of bed. She runs down the hall to investigate the noise. Iggy follows close behind.

First, they check the kitchen. Bunny is there looking around, too.

"What was that noise?" Bunny asks.

The kitchen looks fine. Maybe it was the laundry room? Nope, it's in perfect order.

Penny takes the lead and heads down to the basement. They turn on the light and walk slowly down the stairs. Oh my! They can't believe their eyes. The basement is flooded with water! Penny reaches for a bucket, Iggy grabs some swim gear, and Bunny goes upstairs to call the plumber.

This has been an expensive month for Bunny. First, there was the broken window on the second floor,

then the washing machine overflowed,

then the toilet incident. Wow, what a mess!

"I'm afraid I'm over my spending budget," Bunny sighs.

"Over your budget?" asks Penny.

"Yes, I've spent all the money that I had set aside for repairs," she explains.

Just then, Iggy lets out a big snore.

"Back to bed," says Bunny. "Off you go!"

But Penny tosses and turns. She can't fall asleep. She wants to help Bunny with the repair costs. She needs a big idea, and she'll just have to sleep on it.

The next morning, Penny wakes up with a big idea.

She springs out of bed and announces the plan to Iggy.
"We are going to have our very first jewelry show!"
Iggy rolls over and goes back to sleep.
"Let's go, Iggy!" she says, and yanks him to his feet.

At breakfast, the doorbell rings. It's J.J., the plumber. Bunny takes him down to the basement to assess the damage. "The repairs will cost you one hundred dollars," he says.

Whoa! One hundred dollars is a lot of money. Penny doesn't have that kind of cash! She'll have to work extra hard. She heads up to the Small Mall to check her supplies. She has to make sure she has enough beads, jewels, rings, and string to make jewelry to sell.

She will have to buy more supplies. Penny checks inside her purse to make sure she has her spending wallet. Iggy wants to help, too. He grabs his spending wallet, and they go to the store.

At the craft store, Penny and Iggy go up and down the aisles, putting things in their basket. One by one, Iggy checks off items on their shopping list.

The cashier rings them up. “Your total is ten dollars,” she says.

They each pull five dollars from their spending wallets. Iggy grabs the receipt.

Back at the Small Mall, Penny and Iggy spread their jewelry-making supplies on the table. Penny also found lots of things around the house, like soda tabs that she can use instead of beads. Small pebbles from the garden will make great one-of-a-kind charms, and bird feathers are perfect for funky earrings. She has dreamed up so many designs!

Iggy has his own special designs in mind.

Penny and Iggy get to work. They sleep and eat and work some more.

It takes two days to string the beads, glue the charms, and add all the finishing touches.

And it was worth every minute. What creative designs! Penny prices all the merchandise and carefully arranges it in the Small Mall.

$10.00

The Primo Trunk Show is open for business!

All their hard work is on display. Iggy pats himself on the back.

Neighbors and friends begin arriving one by one. They love the jewelry.

"How darling!"

"How fabulous!"

"These are great!"

"Totally rad!"

Right before closing, Mr. Wilson pops in to buy a necklace for his daughter Maggie. It's the last sale of the day.

Penny sits down to count their earnings. She adds up the sales on a calculator. "Holy moly!" she exclaims when she sees the total. They sold sixty dollars' worth of jewelry.

"But we're not done," explains Penny. "To find out how much money we *really* earned, we have to do a little math.

"Here is the money we made selling jewelry:

$60.00

"Here is the money we spent buying supplies:

$10.00

"Now we subtract the money we spent from the money from sales. This shows us how much money we earned. Wow! We earned fifty dollars!"

"The money we earned is called our PROFIT," explains Penny. "And *that* is what we will give Bunny for the plumbing repairs."

Penny and Iggy head down to look for Bunny. They find her in the basement, knee-deep in water. She could use a helping hand.

"Here," says Penny, giving her the money. "We want to pitch in and help."

They put on their rain boots and jump right in.
"Thank you!" says Bunny. "Every penny helps!
You are both superheroes in my book!"

SUPERHERO
SWAG!

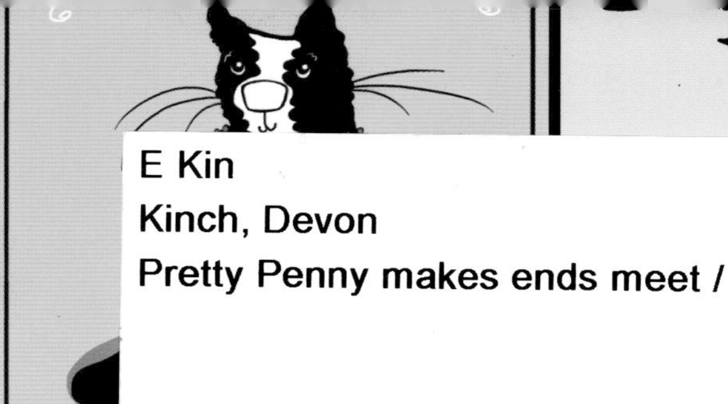

REALLY FABULOUS
FLOWER
RINGS

By
Iggy
SUPERHERO
SWAG!

Pretty Pebble
NECKLACES

Super
Classy
Crowns

REALLY FABULOUS
FLOWER
RINGS

By
Iggy
SUPERHERO
SWAG!

Super
Classy
Crowns

REALLY FABULOUS

By
Iggy